Inside this book:

23 illustrated pages, 10 Foil Art pages, and
4 thin foil transfer sheets enclosed in a pocket inside the cover,
plus a sheet of silver stickers for you to decorate your pictures.

Use pencils and the stickers to complete the pictures on the illustrated
pages. You cannot use the thin foil transfer sheets on these pages.

The Foil Art pages are for you to decorate and embellish
with the foil transfer sheets. Please follow the steps below.

✦ Peel away any of the shaded shapes to reveal a sticky surface.

✦ Rub on a foil sheet of your choice, ensuring the foil's dull side
   is face down on the paper, with the bright side **facing up.**

✦ Gently peel away the foil to reveal your foiled picture.

If you need more foil to complete your Foil Art pictures,
thin foil transfer sheets can be
found at most craft shops.

I could easily learn to prefer an
elephant to any other vehicle.

Mark Twain

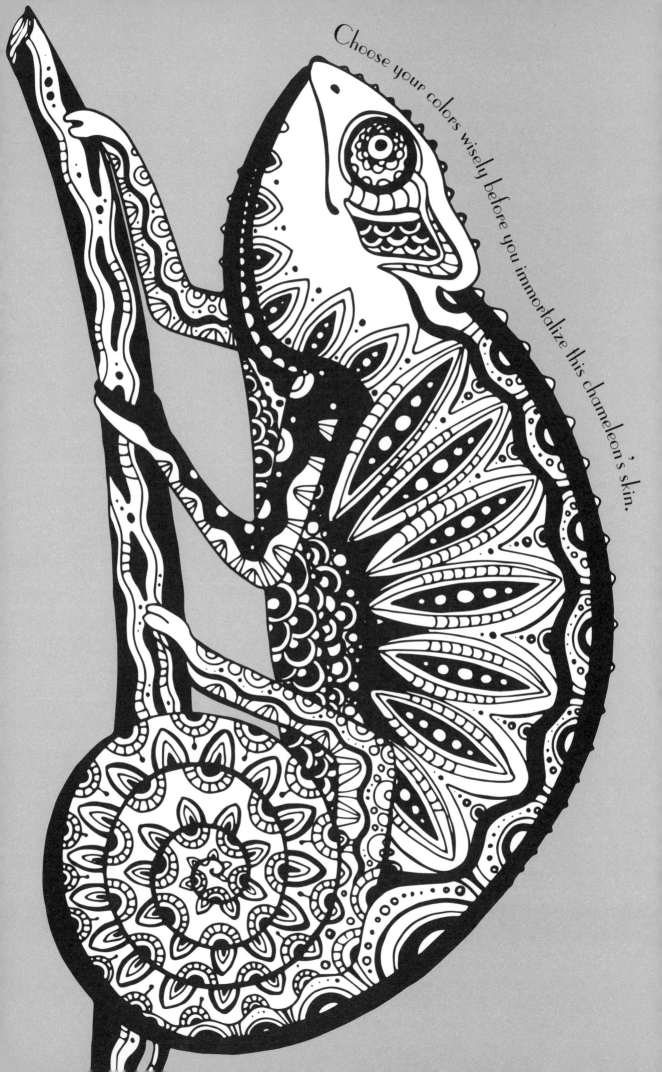

Choose your colors wisely before you immortalize this chameleon's skin.

We never know the love of a parent
till we become parents ourselves.

Henry Ward Beecher

Beware of the boy
who cried wolf.

The butterfly is
a flying flower.

Ponce Denis
Écouchard Lebrun

Color the bobbing seahorse using your most vibrant colors.

"Will you walk into my parlor?"
said the Spider to the Fly.

Mary Howitt

When I bestride him, I soar, I am a hawk: he trots the air;
the earth sings when he touches it.

William Shakespeare

The stag at eve had drunk his fill,
Where danced the moon on Monan's rill.

Sir Walter Scott

Turn this fish into a jewel of the sea by giving each delicate scale a different color.

Transform these intricate patterns with your most striking colors.

Did you think the lion was sleeping
because he didn't roar?

Friedrich Schiller

Soar high with
the majestic eagle.

The fox has many tricks. The hedgehog has but one.
But that is the best of all.

Ralph Waldo Emerson

Dive into the ocean and swim with marine creatures.

"I am Real" said the little Rabbit.
"I am Real! The Boy said so!"

Margery Williams

Help this emperor penguin stand out from the crowd.

What greater gift
than the love of a cat?

Charles Dickens

The armadillo's shell is tough and strong, but that doesn't mean it can't be beautiful.

'Twas the night before Christmas, when all through the house
Not a creature was stirring, not even a mouse.

Clement
Clarke Moore

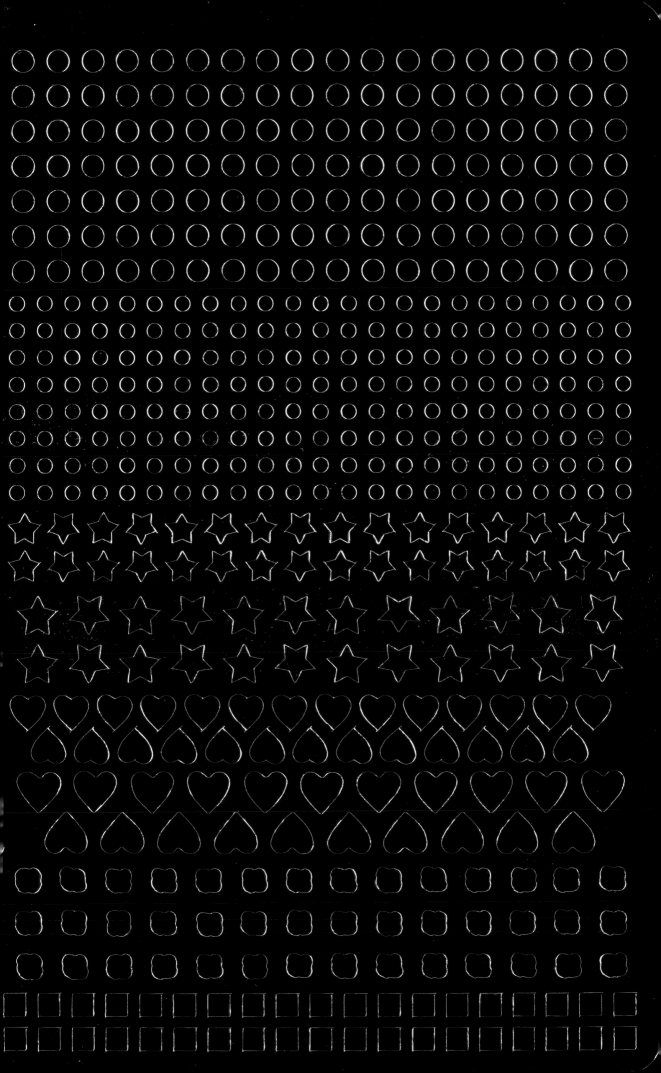